FUNERARY RITES

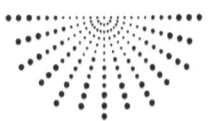

DOUGLAS CLEGG

ALKEMARA
PRESS

SPECIAL EDITION

CONTENTS

FUNERARY RITES

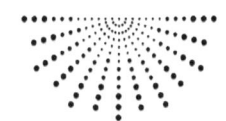

WHAT RUBY SAID

WHEN THE FOREIGNERS FIRST CAME, THEY rented the old Dunwoody place with its rundown barn at the back.

"Coppery people," is how Ruby began her description of them. "The women wear these yellow and blue robes draped like this," she drew her hand over and across her shoulder. "They set everything in straw baskets gently, like putting babies down to sleep. You should have seen the look I got from Jean Marie when I helped them. My *goodness*, you'd have thought I was passing nuclear secrets to the Rosenbergs."

We walked home from her father's store where my wife took afternoon shift three days a week while our son spent time with his aunt. It was one of those warm, unhurried summer evenings from which we stole ten trouble-free minutes together, headaches calmed, hand in hand like kids.

"They say much?"

She shook her head. "Just pointed at things. Held out cash for me to pick and choose from. They've got a smell." Realizing how ugly this sounded, she added, "not unpleasant at all. But unlike anything I've smelled before. Wonder what it is?"

RUBY, whose family went back two hundred years in our village, had never seen three women who looked so different from anyone else in her world.

My wife had grown up within the village terrarium. In some ways, it's why I loved her, particularly after the war, when everything else changed so much. Ruby had retreated in some respects and become more of a small town, old fashioned girl than she'd been when we met.

This is not to say she was ignorant or backward — or even shy. She got her education — a good one — having studied history and art in a local college of pastoral setting, with an ambition of moving *to New York City or even Paris and working in a little gallery or maybe the Metropolitan Museum of Art*, she said within the first twenty minutes of our inaugural conversation, surrounded by a dome of chatter and music.

Who could not fall in love with her?

What a momentous night that was for me:

Imagine if that busload of college girls had not arrived from the state's outer reaches to crash the October tri-collegiate party at Oyster River where dancing went all night and lights were strung like the Milky Way from beam to beam in a barn-sized boathouse.

There, I — morose and undone by my first full month away from home — approached this most compelling girl who stood alone at the edge of everything. She, of soft dark hair and narrow brown eyes hidden beneath the kind of glasses you'd draw off just before you'd kiss her. She was dressed in what looked like her grandmother's cocktail dress with the pelt of a long blue cardigan draped across one shoulder, a magnificent misfit, clutching a bottle of Coca-Cola in one hand as if ready to crack heads with it, a permanently unlit cigarette in the other, not giving a damn about dancing or drinking or whether she looked foolish or not.

"Look around, the world's coming apart at the seams but in here it's all fun and games — and I'd avoid the punch if I were you," Ruby said to me. "I had to be dragged here. What's your excuse?"

"I think I came here to meet you," I said.

RUBY PROBABLY WOULD HAVE LEFT with me after college — and headed off for New York, Paris, or just plain old Boston — had not history both large and small cut short the path.

War intervened the following winter, during which I mainly saw the inside of safe, dusty corridors

3

packed with bespectacled and exacting old men nearly as boring as the work. Flat-footed, four-eyed, color-blind, with a slight hand tremor from birth and an aptitude for numbers and memorization, I was deemed fit more for paperwork than for fighting; I cataloged the missing and the dead.

It became my unenviable job to connect names with numbers and home addresses so that — eventually — a doorbell would be rung and some family stateside given the bad news.

I ran across the names of college friends who had fallen, neighborhood sons who'd been lost in the Pacific, and those possibly dead in the rubble of Europe. I grew to hate the larger world and dream of the kind of village where nobody knew much about what went on out there.

During the first year or two of the war, Ruby and I wrote constantly to each other. The news came from the Pacific that her beloved brother died in combat. In fact, I saw his name on the lists and felt a jab in my heart when I thought of how Ruby would take the news.

Later, when her mother grew sick the letters trickled and then stopped entirely.

She had become moored to her home by that point. Her father needed her, she wrote in her last letter, her sisters couldn't keep the store running, it looked grim for her mother, and Ruby couldn't shake the thought of her older brother dying like that.

And then, the silence.

As soon as I could, I returned, terrified I'd lost my girl to someone else. After I'd located her and spent days in her company, I proposed marriage, imposed pregnancy, and then there was no getting her to up-and-go anywhere else.

For me to be with Ruby, I had to give up the outside world.

At the time, it was how I wanted it. Her hometown remained locked in a dream of what a New England village had always been. The milk was fresh, the air clean, the trees thick with leaf, the streams ice-cold in summer, the neighbors a bit dull, distant yet companionable, friendly in an untrusting way.

After several months, the long lists of the dead vanished from my dreams. I loved my wife and child, I disagreed affably with my father-in-law; we worked, we loved, we played, we ignored; we kept shutters closed in winter and opened our doors wide when spring finally came.

We nestled into village life.

There we were, fairly typical among the locals, more than a decade after our wedding, me at the bank counting other peoples' money and her at the afternoon shift, not ten minutes' walk from where she'd been born, our only child — named for her dead brother — eleven years old the summer that the Smiths arrived.

On that particular walk home, within the first few days of our foreign invasion, I grew inordinately happy.

My wife glimpsed a new horizon in the foreigners and hadn't shrunk from it. In fact, she'd become curious about the newcomers, because "sometimes I feel like a stranger here, too. I don't really think like my father, do I?"

"No," I said. "Not your sisters, either. Or anyone we know. Thank god."

"I think maybe we should travel more," Ruby said on that particular evening, "now that Caleb's older. Aren't you a little bored with things the way they are? I know I am. We could use a breath of fresh air, maybe a change of scenery."

The time had come. We'd hidden too long. Perhaps we'd buy a Chevrolet and drive out west; or do a southern trip; maybe go see Manhattan and tour around a little.

I welcomed the arrival of outside influence in our lives in the form of the Smiths.

At least, I did for awhile.

2

ABOUT THE SMITHS

THE GENERAL SCUTTLEBUTT WENT THAT THEY were a pack of gypsies, then Hindu, Amazonian tribesmen, possibly deposed Mongolian royalty, exiles from Borneo or the Sudan or Burma, terrible Barbary Coast people, islanders of some ruined South Sea paradise — and finally something else entirely that most of us had never heard of.

You might assume we were not the friendliest of villages, but many in town were worried based on the news reports. Immigrants packed Boston, Portsmouth bulged with foreigners, and Manhattan to the far south became a different country entirely.

We never thought outsiders would make it so far inland.

First there were maybe six of them.

Within a week or three, we could count at least fourteen on Main Street on a morning so bright you had to shield your eyes from the sun to make out their crowd hanging around the butcher shop.

Tom Raleigh, who worked the register, told us the foreigners always asked for cuts of meat that nobody ever ate.

"You mean like marrow bones?" Ruby asked.

"Heads," I guessed. "Or hooves."

"No," he said. "I'm not even sure these parts got names. We usually throw that stuff out."

I looked at my wife and she at me, with a crooked, slight smile breaking the calm of her face.

In the pause, Tom added, "it's a little disturbing."

"Well, it's not exactly the end of the world," I said. "I mean, these people seem okay, don't they?"

"Sure," Tom said as he weighed and wrapped up the pork loin we'd have for supper. "I got nothing against them. Nothing at all. I just don't think it's normal. But what do I know? I mean, to each his own."

"I'm going to be up all night wondering what those cuts are," Ruby said on the way out as I held the door open. "It's not like they're cannibals or anything."

"He made it up," I said when we got to our car.

"Now, why would Tom do that?"

I opened the car door for her; she slid in. Once I'd gotten in on the other side, I said, "He's like everyone else. He's got to put his two cents in, have a story about them, spread a little dirt. This town's too damn small."

After that, other strange and unsavory Smith stories began cropping up. Lois Abbott, who ran the library, said Smiths had been stealing books. Paul Lockwood said he caught some of their men peeping through windows at night when most people were asleep. May Peters, at the coffee shop, swore on her father's grave that they went through the trash early in the morning "like a gang of raccoons." Even Helen Cooper — usually less gossipy than most — told my wife she didn't like the way the Smith men eyed teenage girls in town, "like they're sizing up which ones to kidnap as brides."

The Smiths, it was said, held strange celebrations out in the autumn woods accompanied by ghostly chanting and drumbeats "like in *Tarzan*." Two Smith women were seen bare breasted down at the stream, washing sheets against the rocks.

And then some idiot spread the rumor that some Smiths had been caught out at the cemetery "doing voodoo."

You could attach any cockamamie story you wanted to the name Smith, and nine times out of ten, it would stick.

❧

WE CALLED our foreigners the Smiths because nobody could pronounce their names. "Smith" became a joke that we'd never in a million years mention to their faces. Little Smith, Smith Junior, Uncle Smith, Big

Smith, Old Smith, Pretty Smith, Ancient Smith — that kind of thing.

Most of their clan grabbed the lowest rung mill jobs. They never complained these were beneath them or that they were made for better things. They took them happily, and by all accounts, turned the mills around.

We'd see Smiths wandering around on weekends or sometimes early Monday morning. They'd arrive to town in packs of four and five to pick up sundries and fabric or when a big brown trunk arrived from the old country to our post office.

The Smiths didn't drive cars. They used ox-drawn wagons and bicycles. The older ones walked into town clutching hand carved staffs like Biblical shepherds. The elder Smith ladies carried groceries on wooden crossbars at their shoulders or in baskets balanced perfectly on their heads. They'd slowly trudge back — barefoot in summer — to their rented rundown farm, a two mile walk on a blistery afternoon.

You couldn't even offer them rides — I tried once or twice but just got nods and dismissals from the Smith crowd, along with that chattering sound they made when trying to be polite.

At first, we were all proper with the Smiths and respected their customs. You could say — despite the gossip about them — that there existed peace in the land.

But then there was that incident at the cider mill.

THE BATTLE OF DUNWOODY FARM

THE ROWDIER BOYS IN THE VILLAGE CLAIMED A Smith started it.

The boys who raised the flag and ran up the hill mainly came from the Crocker family, six tawny-haired scoundrels between the ages of 12 and 17, all of them destined for prisons in some distant future, all of them getting away with their crimes (stealing a few sawbucks from a till, spying on a local Venus in her bath, egg-fights along Main Street, a window shot through, the murdered parakeet incident, the famous joyride in a jalopy ending in a crash and tumble, whisperings of girls-in-trouble leaving town under mysterious circumstances).

There were others, too, the sheep-boys who followed the bad ones. These little disciples were as guilty; and yes, I counted my own son in that. Caleb had turned twelve at the time with just enough rambunctiousness in his blood to do the wrong thing.

The boys of the village first threw hard, green apples like grenades; then the warm pies sitting out along cooling shelves; finally rocks and marbles and anything that could gain velocity between fist and back-of-head.

The Smith boys — most of them under the age of fifteen — fought back, of course, but with less dumb luck.

A skirmish ensued, war declared. What began at the cider mill ended with a chase out to the Dunwoody farm. Cows fled their pen, chickens flew, windows smashed, a threshold trespassed.

A flaming arrow made it into a barn window and someone — I suspected Paul Lockwood's kid — dumped manure in the well.

After the whuppings — and there were several — we all made our sons apologize.

It was quite a spectacle: twenty boys of varying shape and size, prodded forward by their fathers in a kind of Death March through town, out along the little bridge over the stream that went to the Dunwoody place.

Their heads hung low, they scratched at imagined itches, some hands clasped in droopy prayer or slow hand-wringing, some (mainly those Crocker boys) cast sidelong glances to the fields beyond the stone walls as if plotting escape routes.

My boy Caleb bowed his head and said he was sorry to every single Smith, though he only marginally participated in the fracas and received not a single belt to his behind. Still, I gave him a good talking to and there'd be no privileges for a good long while.

He had, I told him, better damn straighten up before he ended up like a Crocker.

The kids cleaned up their mess. An offering of cash for repairs. A calf given as a gift. A fence mended. We — of the Selectmen — got out and repaired the barn.

The Smiths themselves quickly offered the olive branch, spoke slowly and formally in a language none of us understood but I guessed was their way of telling us to put it in the past and leave them alone and please — in their eyes a sliver of fear — *don't ever bother us again.*

A cloud came over our town that day and remained.

We felt ashamed of our sons' behaviors. We didn't like the idea that we'd become the bad neighbors. We preferred to think of foreigners as a kind of benign tumor to be watched for signs of malignancy.

We were not arrogant people. We liked to live in peace. We didn't nurture disagreements, though they existed. We didn't want to get involved in conflicts with any foreigners. We'd heard that some towns created battle lines with their own versions of the Smiths and sometimes this ended in terrible consequence for everybody.

TURNS OUT, in their exuberant and uncalled-for

attack, our boys managed to desecrate some sacred cow or other.

Young Smith — one of the eldest of their boys — explained the whole thing to me in halting English without actually naming our sacrilege.

A blasphemy had occurred. Our boys had no idea what they'd really done. Young Smith told us that their women stopped eating because of it. Two middle-aged Smiths had to leave at once — at great expense — for the journey to the motherland to offer propitiation. Offerings were being burnt even as we were informed of this.

We had crossed into the territory of taboo and Young Smith warned us that the older men of his tribe wept with this injustice, a strong-hearted young man lost his left hand in a mill accident and a young wife miscarried twins with misshapen limbs, among other signs of tribal apocalypse.

"This house is no longer holy," Young Smith told us. "It is a place of darkness to us now. We must avoid a war."

A war?

Foreigners! Invaders! War!

All the things we didn't want in our little off-the-beaten-track borough.

Later, at our town meeting, we scratched our heads and came up with possibilities of which line had been crossed. Was it the hay that burned in the barn? The well? The escaped cow? Someone even suggested it might be that apples were sacred to whatever hundred gods and goddesses the heathens worshipped.

Or the pies?

We never figured it out, but nobody wanted to start a war — "their word not ours" — with the Smiths because "nobody knows where that'll end."

The lowest of our minds — and we had more than our share — imagined machetes, spears, little knives, or shrunken heads all in a row.

The Smiths moved a little further out of town.

For their new tribal home, the Smiths grabbed the big house at the edge of the marsh.

❧

MALVERN HOUSE — enormous and colonial and crumbly — was somewhat hidden from an untrammeled dirt road behind high stone walls and jagged trees. The marsh stench was impossible to avoid. Who else would choose to live there but outsiders?

My friend, Cormac Danielson, their landlord and a man who owned several dilapidated properties in the deep woods, took some heat over this rental, a few nasty looks by the harsher folk in the village, but most of us didn't care. Few ever traveled that road, no one hunted at the marshes anymore, it was a dead end off an out-of-the-way half-past a nowhere. The place came surprisingly cheap and held a good twelve bedrooms — perfect for the Smiths — and not a single indoor toilet.

By then, there were at least twenty of them living at Malvern, all loosely related, most coming down the matriarchal side from the old lady we called Ancient Smith.

Twenty became forty. More Smiths arrived over a two year period.

One winter, they bought Malvern House for what was reportedly a tidy sum. Well of course, some people said, they could buy it and the damn marsh and even the fields around it when they lived forty to a house and they all took the mill jobs away from more deserving people. They'd been moving up in their jobs, and rumor went that one of them was about to make an offer on the paper mill.

"They're going to own us all soon enough, just watch," Paul Lockwood said, though we all laughed at the time.

Local boys — expressly warned to never bother the Smiths again — reported strange goings-on out there. Wild animal cries. Smells of strange spice and odd bonfires along the marsh. Music played on weird drums, screechy fiddles that sounded like mating cats and oddly shaped clarinets that produced even odder whines. Lights in the sky. Bizarre sounds of strangulation that might pass for singing.

Paul Lockwood began calling Malvern House the city of foreign relations by the time my boy turned fifteen. People eventually forgot that it was ever called Malvern House and instead, it became known as Smithville.

By then, they owned the paper mill and had bought one hundred fifty acres of woodland along the river, including the old Shalcross farm. A much larger Smith settlement arose, and the boundaries of Smithville continued nudging out along the county line.

We pretty much stayed away from them, and they — in turn — kept their distance.

Until something happened to change it all.

4

THE COFFEE SHOP DEBATE

ONE SUMMER MORNING, THE OLDEST SMITH BOY came riding his bicycle to town.

He was tall and scrawny and wore only a cloth at his waist. He dropped the bike in the street and went running up to Dr. Knowles' office, across from the bank where I worked. The kid shouted so much that we all went to the windows to watch as the doctor stepped out and exchanged a few words with the boy. Then, Dr. Knowles went back inside.

The boy paced, striking the air with his fists. He glanced over at those of us watching. The look on his face was devastating — tears streamed down his face, his mouth open and sagging, his eyes pleading.

"Something bad's happened with those people," one of the bank tellers said.

Dr. Knowles came out to the street, spoke with the boy, put his hand on the boy's shoulder. They left together in the doctor's sleek Chrysler.

It was the first time — to any of our knowledge — that a Smith sat in a car seat.

This became a topic of interest down at the coffee shop where several of us watched the Chrysler return and park across the street, just after the work day had ended.

Dr. Knowles, noticing our stares as he got out of his car, came striding over.

Once inside the coffee shop, he called an informal meeting of the Selectmen.

This was easily accomplished because we were all sitting around with half-drunk cups of coffee in our hands.

·

"THE OLD LADY'S so sick, I wanted to put her out of her misery," Dr. Knowles told our group when we'd pushed tables together and gathered with our lemonades and coffees and pastries. "They don't believe in hospitals. And it doesn't matter — she won't make it to one. I got her as comfortable as anyone can be in that condition."

He stirred his coffee and looked down into it as if it were a crystal ball. "She'll be dead by tomorrow."

"Terrible," I said.

Ruby sat opposite me, next to Helen Cooper, whose husband Josh — my closest friend in town — was to my left. Paul Lockwood sat to my right, while

Dr. Knowles had squeezed in between Willie Crocker and Dave Neary at table's end.

"Awful," Ruby said. "I feel as if I just saw her at the store last Wednesday. She's old but I didn't think…"

"As weepy as this is," Paul Lockwood said. "What's it got to do with any of us?"

"They need to perform funerary rites," Dr. Knowles said.

"Sounds heathen," Paul grumbled.

"Well, everybody has customs," the doctor said. "And they have a particular way they bury their dead in that country."

"But they're not in that country."

Dr. Knowles laid out the basics:

"The boy told me his family fasts for three days. There's some holy man of theirs in Manhattan who will come up. Preparations may take a full week. The body stays above ground. They say prayers night and day. The women cover themselves in ash and the men will wear nothing but a plain cloth around their waists. No one washes until after a customary period. The children won't speak during sunlit hours. There are a few less savory aspects to the customs, but there's no need to talk about it here. By week's end, they'll have a feast — and even games."

"I assume this won't be like the Olympics," Willie Crocker joked.

"Sounds heathen," Paul Lockwood groaned. "I

mean, I'm not saying it's wrong. I hate to judge people, but it sounds so damn heathen."

We all looked across the table at him.

"Never seen you in church," I said.

"Church is for hypocrites and sinners," Paul said.

Dr. Knowles continued, "The son took off immediately. There's a larger community of his mother's relatives over in Boston. They have a whole process to this. It's very regulated, I suppose. Now, I may not agree with it but I know these people. I know how hurt — and angry — they'll be if we can't accommodate this one night."

I shrugged. "Let them do whatever they want out there."

The doctor offered an inscrutable look. "It's more involved than that."

A few among us muttered things, but I kept my eyes on Dr. Knowles' face.

"Drop the other shoe," I said.

He rubbed his eyes. The man was exhausted.

"They need to parade her through our streets," he said.

"That's necessary?" Paul Lockwood jumped in. "A *parade*?"

"This was their matriarch," the doctor said. "She's sort of — well, I suppose you'd call her a queen of their tribe. She gets a royal procession."

"Like Fourth of July?" Dave Neary said.

"Maybe we should roll out a red carpet," Paul Lockwood said. "Bow down. Pray to their gods."

21

"Damn Smiths," Willie Crocker said. "They should just take the boat back to where they come from."

Dr. Knowles sighed. "This is no different than our funerals. You go along the streets, the hearse, all that. If this were our President, or even the Governor..." He looked around at the rest of us. Then at me, as if I might help convince the others.

"Sure," I said to our group. "It's a little unusual. But it's not like we didn't go all out when Vernon Browne kicked off a few years back."

"Not the same thing," Willie Crocker said. "He was an American war hero."

"I don't see why we need to let them bring their customs here," Helen said, avoiding all our looks.

"We were here first," Willie Crocker said. "When those Smiths have lived here for two hundred years, then they can have some say in this."

"I have nothing against them. Honestly," Helen said. "But they don't live in the village."

"They buy from us," Ruby said. "They bank here. I mean, I'd hate to lose their business, Helen. Wouldn't you? The store's grown because of them. They could just as easily go to Remington or Hazelford if they had to, and I'd hate to think of the money we'd lose, if nothing else."

"I'm telling you, it's heathen," Paul Lockwood said for the umpteenth time, and on went the arguments.

"Here's the part that'll be a tough sell for our neighbors, I'm sure," Dr. Knowles interrupted our debate. "They have rules to this procession. No one can look at them. We have to draw curtains, close shutters. Not a single person in town — man, woman, child or dog — can be on the street. It's that sacred."

We all took this in.

"How long's this shindig going to last?" I asked.

"It'll start right at sundown and run until dawn I think. He told me it's involved. It'll be noisy, too."

"Primitives," Paul Lockwood said. "Wailing, caterwauling, no doubt chanting."

"It's a cult," Josh Cooper said. "I don't mind them, but I don't really like the idea of this." He leaned in to me. "I mean, do you? Why do they even need to come through our village? Can't they stay out on their own land?"

The table went silent.

May Peters brought the coffee pot over and refilled our cups. She apologized for eavesdropping, "but whenever I hear about the Smiths, I just can't help it."

"May?" I asked.

"I've never liked them," she said.

"You ain't alone, sister," Willie said.

"They're not so bad," Ruby said. "If you give them a chance."

Truth was, they weren't bad at all; and yet, in my deepest self, I had to admit that I'd never been quite comfortable around the Smiths. They'd kept themselves so separate over the years that it was as if our own culture had been rejected by them as not worthy. I wasn't smart enough to explore why this bothered me, but it *did* bother me. This seemed at the root of all our unease.

They had never quite accepted *us*.

As if we hadn't heard her the first time, May repeated, "I've just never liked them and I'm not afraid to say it out loud."

Dr. Knowles looked up at her. "It's not a matter of 'like'. They're part of our town. They've hurt no one. They deserve our respect — and compassion — in this situation."

"They smell different," May said. "They cook strange stuff, too."

"My wife cooks strange stuff," I said, and Ruby reached over to swat the air in front of my face in mock anger.

"Close our curtains? That's ridiculous. I won't do it," May said as she receded into the coffee shop while her voice grew louder. "What are we supposed to do? Not go outside, not even look at the stars? Skip any kind of night out we might have planned? Who does that? Is everything supposed to shut down at nine o'clock for them? For those people?"

After May mumbled away, Dr. Knowles lowered his voice. "A lot of people are going to feel like that. Look, we must convince everyone to do this. The Smiths believe that if even one outsider sees the funeral parade, terrible things will happen. World-changing things, he said. For all of us."

"Like what?" Willie asked, a kind of backwoods challenge in his voice.

Dr. Knowles shrugged. "We really want to find out?"

"Maybe they'll set us on fire," Paul muttered. "They like their fires, those heathens."

"This *is* their Queen. And frankly," Dr. Knowles tilted his head slightly as if convincing himself, "they outnumber us."

There, someone had finally said it. More than three hundred Smiths occupied farmland and woodland, and our little village didn't quite hit that number. If you needed any kind of factory job, you probably worked *with* or *for* at least one of the Smith clan. If you worked over in Hazelford, where the great jobs tended to be, you had to drive twenty miles across Smith land to get there.

Dr. Knowles had said the one thing that none of the rest of us wanted to examine:

We didn't really run things in quite the same way as we once had. Oh, we ran the village, no doubt, and we were like the villages in all directions, but in terms of population, the Smiths had us beat.

At the table, we chewed the subject a bit more, but agreed with Dr. Knowles in the final minutes before heading home.

We'd call an emergency town meeting to make this happen.

Then, after a night of shouting matches in the old meeting hall that went late into the night, we exhausted opponents of this proposal into offering just this one summer night to the Smith family and to no one else.

It was in the town's best interest.

One night we heard the sound of a strange horn — deep and sonorous — and knew that the funeral had begun.

5

THE FUNERAL PARADE

Sunset brushed the trees with a rusty haze. Within an hour or two, we all should've been heading to bed anyway but…well, who could sleep once they thought of the entire Smith clan and some strange priest of their cult walking down Main Street?

We anticipated some unavoidable indecency in the request to close our eyes to their dark celebration. It gave a little thrill to the quiet summer night.

Before drawing the final curtain in the front hall, I glanced out into the shadowed street and saw that all the neighboring homes were shuttered.

The village — from what I could see —shut down tight as a clam.

I closed the curtain.

❦

THE INSIDE of our home became toasty to the point where we'd all stripped down to shorts and undershirts and my wife wore only a slip once we'd sent Caleb up to his room.

Josh Cooper kept calling me: had they come 'round yet? Did anyone see them?

And I kept telling him to forget it and just go to bed.

I sat in the living room watching Ruby pace back and forth as if expecting a guest at the door. Now and then, she'd look over and say, "I don't know why I'm so keyed up," or "you'd think I'd just read a book and go to bed, but I'm almost afraid."

"It's the heat," I said. "Look, if you'd just sit. Drink some lemonade. You'll cool down."

"It's not the heat," she said, "although my god, these fans do nothing without the windows open."

I pointed out the three windows that were in fact open, particularly the ones facing the garden. "And we have six fans going. It's not that bad."

"And the noise. Someone should invent a quiet fan. It's like living inside a beehive," she said. "I'm hoping they come through fast. I can maybe take an hour of this. Maybe not even an hour."

"Take a cool shower," I said.

"It is *not* the heat," Ruby said. "And I don't need a shower."

Caleb, expressly forbidden to look out his shuttered window, had gone to bed — reluctantly — early, with a book he'd been supposed to read all summer, although my wife and I heard his radio on upstairs playing rock n roll over the hum of fans.

"Any other night, I'd yell for him to turn it down," I said.

Ruby ignored my comment.

"You think anyone will look?" Ruby asked. "I mean, how will they not? You're told not to do something, you do it. It's human nature."

"God, I hope not."

"It's not as if the Smiths'll notice," she said. "Jeanne Marie told me she was going to peek. But only a little. There's that dormer window with a little bit of the shutter missing and she said she and Bill would sit up just for a look."

"They shouldn't risk it," I said. Then I swore. "Everybody promised they wouldn't look. I hope Jeanne Marie was just pulling your leg."

"Well it's not as if the Smiths'll see them. And that's all we need to do. Make sure they don't see us looking."

"Is it so hard to just not look outside for one night? How often do we come home, have supper and then not even glance out the open window?"

"This is different."

"How so?"

"It's like being in prison," she said. "Or a coffin."

Ruby stopped pacing. She went and sat on the rug by the coffee table. She picked up a copy of *Reader's*

Digest and read off all the article titles in a droning voice and then put it down again. She drew her knees to her chin, reminding me of a girl I once knew. Her long tan legs, the silky slip, the way her shoulders shrugged and her hair swept across half her face. She had never looked more appealing to me. Where was that girl with the Coke bottle in one hand, the cigarette in the other, the glasses and old-fashioned dress that I'd first met? Replaced now by this siren, a dream of slip and girl and desperation.

"Come here, you," she said.

"Honey?"

"Come here." She held her arms out. I went over and crouched down in front of her.

She drew me into the cradle of her body. We were sweaty and there was something filthy about her wanting me like that. I felt as if I were taking advantage of her.

I pulled back, and we sat there staring at each other.

"I know, I know," she moaned. "I just wanted to get away from all this. Can't we get away?"

I felt confused by this state she was in.

"It's okay," I said. "We can go upstairs if you want."

"No," she said. "It's like I want a pill or a drink."

"What a compliment."

"You know what I mean. I just want to block it out."

I returned to the chair and she stood up and began pacing again.

"I didn't think I'd feel like this," she said. "All jittery. It's like the world's going to end or something."

"I promise you the world won't end."

"I mean, they could've picked Hazelford. They've got that farm by the river. Why us? It's strange. It's just too strange."

She stomped her feet, just a little, a spoiled girl instead of a woman in her thirties.

"What's gotten into you?"

"I don't know," she said. "I don't know. But all I think is, you go along in life the way you're supposed to, you do all the right things, all the things that make a good life. You marry, start a family, raise your kid, work a job, go to church, honor your father, be nice to everybody, and then one night you're in a closed up house with every door locked up and you can't even look outside because you're somehow not good enough. It's how I feel right now, and I know it sounds crazy, but when I think of my brother Caleb dying on some foreign island and my mother dying in her bed and thinking I'd lost you until you came back and then how things changed so quickly here and how I've been afraid to…"

I had to catch my breath as she went on and on. I'd never heard my wife talk like this. She dug up tales from her childhood, from our own past, some argument we had, the miscarriage after Caleb, the fact that I hadn't fought in the war but pushed papers while her brother had given the ultimate sacrifice, the idea of wifedom and what it meant, and sisterdom and daughterdom and motherhood and how fathers expected so much and how she'd given up chances because of the stupid war and all these women in town who made comments about your house and wallpaper and how much your husband made and how you dressed and all the stupid things she'd had to do because it was like following a rule book.

Her nose ran and spit flew in the middle of this rough waterfall of words and she stood over me flailing her arms around. I felt somehow responsible. She didn't shout, she just let this stream flow from her. She grew all teary-eyed. Sweat burst along her forehead. She went off on me and the world and everything she'd never mentioned before in her life.

I honestly wondered if she might be having a nervous breakdown.

Only then did I notice that our son's radio had gone silent upstairs.

My wife and I stared at each other in the buzz of many fans. I patted my lap. Calming, perhaps exhausted, she sat down and we cuddled, but I could tell that this wasn't enough. We were sweaty, uncomfortable, dissatisfied.

Just get through this one night, I thought. *She feels boxed in. It's the heat. It's the idea that we're not as free as we thought we were. That's all. She'll be fine in the morning.*

"You do everything right," she whispered as if in a

confessional. "But it doesn't matter. You give up dreams. You do things so other people will think you're fine. You don't take risks because if you risk things, you lose. People you love might die. The world might fall apart. But nothing you do adds up. None of it makes sense."

I thought about how maybe we should've taken those trips we'd planned — to the Grand Canyon or to St. Augustine or even just to Manhattan to see the museums.

We'd let life get in the way.

The phone rang. She got out of my lap.

"Where you headed?"

Ruby glanced back at me and for a second I thought she wouldn't answer.

"Honey?" I said.

"I think I'll take that shower."

I reached for the phone.

"THAT YOU?" It was Josh.

"Who else?"

"Hear the music yet?"

"No."

"It'll get louder when it gets to your side. Believe me."

A pause on the line.

"You better not be looking," I said.

"I just snuck a peek out the attic window. Over

the rooftops to where the road veers into town. And you wouldn't believe it."

"I don't want to hear about it. Just shut the curtains, go to bed, or go work in your basement or something."

"Hell with that. You should see it. Torches lighting everything up like it's the middle of the day practically. And Elephants! Camels! A wagon — no, more like a golden chariot, drawn by tigers! It's like the circus — or Cleopatra — coming to town. There must be a hundred or more of them — not all of them Smiths, either — waving incense around, twirling sabers and dancing. The men in robes, the women wrapped up like mummies but some of them — hold on to your hat — don't got nothin' on from the waist up."

"Quit looking," I said.

"All of 'em moving this way and that, a big guy blowing this bull's horn and a bunch of women playing some kind of flute. Bunch of little boys running around smashing cymbals together. Two guys wearing big antlers, some of them painted all in gold and silver. And then there's Mr. and Mr. Smith…"

"Wait, you're *still* watching?"

"Pretty much."

"Stop it."

"Look, you've got to see this — they have crowns on. Golden crowns with glittering jewels. Like it's the sultan and his queen or something. And that oldest boy of theirs? He's got this big pole and at its top it looks like a golden snake all wrapped around it. He has flowers all over him, head to toe, and maybe a dozen half-naked girls following after him like he's the catch of the day."

"Shut it," I said.

"You've just got to look out a window. Wait, they're going around, over near your place," he said. "I'm telling you, you have never in all your days seen something like this and I'm guessing you never will again. You miss this, you miss everything."

I hung up the phone.

I argued with my better nature: we promised, this is their ritual, this is their custom, honor them, they're good neighbors, Josh exaggerated anyway, how could camels and elephants and tigers be all together here?

They weren't even from a country of camels and elephants and tigers after all, why would they have them?

Had they raided a zoo? Rented from Ringling Brothers?

But it drove me a bit crazy.

I went over to the living room window. *I might just move the curtain slightly. Just a quarter inch. Just enough to see out.*

I began to hear the music. The cymbals, the flutes, the beat of the drums, the strange string instruments that whined and screeched. If I stepped away from the curtains, our fans drowned out the sounds. But right up next to the window…

The Smith noise grew louder in my head.

My fingers brushed the curtain's edge.

Don't do it, I thought. *What if they see you?*

Josh Cooper already risked a possible skirmish by spying from his attic. How many more in town would break their promise?

❧

"YOU'RE LYING. OR JOKING," I said when I called Josh back.

"No," he said. "You need to look out there. They'll never see you. They're too involved in their…well, their spectacle. I saw three little girls riding some kind of large wild pig. I've never seen anything like it. And all these banners. And colored paper. And blankets with spirals and things all over them. And lights, these amazing lights."

"What about the coffin?"

"Coffin? What? Oh, no, it's not like that. They must not believe in that. Ancient Smith. The Queen. You should see. It's as if she's still alive. They have her raised up in this silver chair of some kind and she's dressed like she's going to a wedding, all bright scarves and bracelets. It really is something to see, you should just look, just for a second."

I went silent. I'd heard a noise from upstairs.

"Got to go." I hung up. I bounded up the stairs, thinking I'd check on Ruby in the shower. Halfway up, I saw Caleb crouched in the hall by the narrow window, his head beneath the shade.

"What do you think you're doing?"

36

He bumped his head on the glass. The paper shade slapped him as he ducked back from under it.

When Caleb turned around he couldn't look me in the eye.

"Sorry, dad."

"Go to your room."

"But dad, you got to see it. There's this…"

"Stop right there, young man." I pointed at him as if throwing a lightning bolt. "You know the rules tonight."

"They'll never see me," he said. "And there's this bird — I think it's a bird — it's huge and clomping around. And one of the Smith kids is riding it just like a horse."

"Really?" I asked, losing my fatherly power for a moment.

"Just look for a second," my boy said.

"We promised we wouldn't."

"They'll never know."

"It's *honor*, Caleb," I said and then shooed him to his room at the back of the house.

I wanted to peer under the shade, but resisted.

Instead, I went to check on Ruby. I knocked on the bathroom door and heard her say, "just a minute," so I waited on the landing. I kept glancing over at the shade, wondering if my sense of duty was getting in the way of seeing something truly remarkable.

After awhile, the water still running — Ruby loved her long showers — I went to our bedroom. I lay down in the dark and listened to the strange music outside.

I closed my eyes.

At some point in the night, I heard our front door slam shut.

I got up and went downstairs, thinking someone might be breaking in.

The door wasn't completely closed.

Someone had gone outside.

Who?

I peered out the front window, nearly trembling, thinking that I was doing something awful.

The parade was still going but the drums had stopped their incessant beating. I saw flashes of it: large bears walking on hind legs, a woman riding a chariot drawn by tigers, several children carrying sparklers, wide hoops being tossed in the air and caught again as they landed effortlessly in young men's hands, the colorful robes, the elephants, the dancing women, the children playing cymbals and flutes, a long chain of dancers as the Smiths performed their rites all night through our village.

Among them, I caught a glimpse of my son.

Caleb was shirtless and had painted his chest in bright colors as he danced around with various young Smiths. Helen Cooper — with silk of various shades drawn over her — rode atop the elephant with others from our village, and there was Young Smith and Child Smith and Girl Smith and Middle-Age Smith, and then wonder of wonders, Paul Lockwood, too, part of this strange procession. Running after them, grabbing the hand of one of the Smith uncles, May Peters leapt up to a platform carried by several Smiths and began dancing. I worried about the idea of feuds and bad blood and thought of terrible futures for us, for the Smiths, for our village and its mostly placid surface.

I felt a sudden urge to join in the festivities, but I remained worried: what would become of us? Would the Smiths forgive those who did?

Or would we pay a heavy price for breaking this rule?

World-changing things, Dr. Knowles had said.

I couldn't run out there. I couldn't just go grab Caleb. I'd cause more of a problem, create a greater sacrilege.

Better just to leave it. Pretend you saw nothing.

These are the things I considered in my three a.m. weariness.

I wasn't even sure if I might actually still be in bed dreaming. I had that half-awake, half-somewhere-else feeling the whole time.

When I went back to bed, I noticed that Ruby was not there, on the other side. There wasn't even an indent in the pillow where her head would have rested.

Probably sleeping downstairs in the den, I thought. Sometimes she did. Sometimes I snored. Sometimes, she told me, she couldn't stand my heat when we lay there together in the middle of the night.

I WOKE up later than usual.

I checked Caleb's room. My unease turned to panic when I went downstairs and could not find my wife.

Damp footprints went from the bathroom to the front door, which was open wide to the street.

When I stepped out onto the front porch, I noticed several of the other houses across from us with their doors open wide, too.

BY THE END of the day, those left in town could only guess what happened.

"Dr. Knowles said we'd been warned," Josh said, when I stopped by his hardware store. "And they shouldn't have looked."

"I doubt that's all that happened," I said. "I mean, we both looked. We didn't join in."

"I didn't even think Helen so much as peeked," he said. "She was going a little crazy last night. It was so hot. She got angry that any of us agreed to their terms. But I didn't think…"

"Yeah, Ruby was sort of like that, too," I said.

I imagined Ruby, watching from the bathroom window.

The long cold shower, walking out, dancing, being lifted up onto one of their chariots.

"Why *them* and not us?" Josh said on another day when we'd gotten used to what happened the night of the parade. "Why'd Helen run out there like a kid heading for the ice cream truck? I mean, I saw it happen and I knew — I just *knew* — that if I stepped outside the door, I'd end up with the Smiths, too."

"Maybe they were missing something over here," I said, looking down into my hands. "Who knows?"

And another afternoon, work day done, in the coffee shop:

"Don't worry. They'll come back," Josh said, patting me on the shoulder. "I mean, living in Smithville? It's not what they're used to. The weather'll turn. It won't seem so exciting. They'll miss comforts. They'll wake up and wonder, *what the hell was I thinking?* I mean, I can't even imagine Helen without modern plumbing. I doubt she'll make it to October. And then they'll return home, tails between legs, the village'll get back to its business and we'll forgive and forget. We'll all look back on this summer as one of those odd things, like when the Crash happened, or when Pearl Harbor got hit, like we think it'll never be normal again, but you know, after awhile, it just goes back to being what it always was."

"Sure," I said. "They'll come back."

6

RUBY SIGHTINGS

A NEW FEAR OF THE SMITHS OVERTOOK OUR village. What else might they take? What further revenge would they exact? How much did we really know about them and what they were capable of?

We had weapons — some of us said — we can go free our children and husbands and wives at gunpoint; but no one picked up a gun because on some deep level we feared that the Smiths held a power greater than even bullets.

Or worse, that our loved ones wouldn't want to return to the lives they'd had. They might prefer instead the many hearths of Smithville.

Now and then, those of us who remained behind would drive out to their settlements to catch a glimpse of someone we'd lost.

I saw my boy Caleb — by then, seventeen — standing at a window at the old Malvern place. His face was painted in streaks of whitewash and blue. He wore a mottled blue and green robe wrapped over his shoulder like a toga. He held a little baby in his arms.

When I waved, he didn't seem to recognize me.

Caleb had their look — that Smith gaze, a strangely placid expression, a kind of flat affect as if he were living in a different world beneath his skin.

I tried to trap my son once or twice. He became docile when I locked him up. He wouldn't eat. He'd start chanting in that foreign language — a doleful bleating.

I had to let him go. What was the use? I didn't want to take the risk that he'd starve to death in his father's house or that I'd end up causing something worse to happen.

I watched as he rode his old bicycle back to Smithville.

I began to stay indoors, mostly. I shuttered the windows every night, stopped listening to the news, went to bed early, woke up late, did my job, said the expected things, and hoped for the best.

Others ran into Ruby now and then.

I'd ask them not to speak of her so much, not to me, not anymore. "She's not who she was," I'd say or else, "She's made her choice," or "I guess I never really knew her at all. How well do we really know anyone?"

If only, I'd think.

If she'd just stayed inside, just kept the curtain closed, just done what was asked.

Friends told me about how good Ruby looked, but also how strange, how different, how similar, as if

Ruby had been copied by the Smiths and the real Ruby no longer existed, not the Ruby they'd known their whole life, anyway.

How she didn't seem to recognize them at all when they tried talking to her. How she refused their offers of lifts or escorts or their whispered pleas to come back to town.

How Ruby would move past them, after a Saturday morning's errand, her hair long again, sometimes braided, her skin a deep rich summer tan, a crossbar yolk on her shoulders, carrying baskets of groceries or piles of colored fabric.

She walked barefoot — they said — and not too far behind a few of the other Smith ladies.

AFTERWORD

I believe it's a mistake for a writer to explain much to a reader about a story. It's up to the reader to decide.

But hey, I'll make many mistakes in this life and I accept that.

So here goes.

❦

I wrote *Funerary Rites* from a sense of despair over the often-irrational fears that have plagued humankind throughout history, particularly the unfounded fears over what is alien or other.

On a smaller and more personal scale, I've experienced both sides of this fear in my life. I wanted to express an aspect, via story having nothing to do with my own version of this, in these characters that came to me.

This subject is ripe for horror and dystopian

stories. What it masks, I believe, is the mind's inability to grasp a real threat versus an imagined one.

These fears dovetail with our nightmares and sense of security — of which there may be none, as any sparrow or mouse or even coyote would tell you:

There's only the daily struggle to get through it all with a song or a squeak or a howl of joy on occasion.

I loved writing these characters.

People appear in terms of faces, often when I'm on the cliff edge of falling asleep. These are folks I've never met wearing expressions that make me wonder about what they've seen and done and where they're going.

Some are grotesque, some nightmarish, some beautiful. Most of them seem ordinary faces in a crowd.

Ruby, in particular, appeared one night.

I feel as if she's the center of the story. What we do know about her is that the narrator met her when both were young and she was unusual among the crowd. And then her life closes up a bit, because of a war, and it gets smaller, and fear enters.

Ruby mirrors the frustrations of life spent doing the right thing, living the right way by other peoples' standards, all the while the world can be a careless wreck.

Her longing for something else, buried, erupts in a choice.

Or is she coerced?

Is it some strange witchcraft that entices her to these Smiths and their primitive ways?

But there is this other life that can be lived. That's what the Smiths represented to me as I wrote the story.

While some in town may perceive a growing threat, what are the Smiths doing, after all?

It's what we all want to do. Take care of ourselves and our surroundings, work hard for the good of our families, keep life simple in some ways, honor our dead with the celebration of a circus parade…

Maybe I'm the only one who wants to do *that* in particular. When I die, please bring out the dancing young people, the cymbals, the elephants and alpaca and what-have-you.

Parade my corpse around town just to annoy the neighbors.

Then, burn my detritus on the shore of a dark lake.

Blow my ashes in the faces of mine enemies.

Or some such.

You know what?

I don't know everything about what I write, and you may have concluded an entirely different thing and created a story from my story that is further along in its insight than I can be and has nothing to do with a face seen on the edge of a dream.

So, don't listen to me.

❦

After I've finished writing books or stories, I usually try and find the earliest genealogy of the type of story sitting before me.

This allows me to confirm that what I've written about is likely not just true for me, but resonates and connects. The essence of story echoes through various permutations going back hundreds or thousands of years. Show me any story that readers respond to, and I'll find its genealogy in stories of the distant past.

May take me awhile, but I'll find it.

I am an unapologetic lover of stories great and small so long as they ring true in some way even if not realistic ways — since realism is its own kind of fiction.

My loves in reading are, both academically and personally, classical literature and popular fiction, but I've been immersing in all this stuff since childhood, as well as fairy tale, world mythology, ancient drama, poetry, and so on.

All of which I constantly re-read because…it's fun for me to do.

I found after writing *Funerary Rites* that the earliest genealogy I can attach to it was simply the story of the "Pied Piper." (Possibly a bit of the Lady Godiva legend or even the "Artemis offended in her woodland bath while Actaeon peeks" story in at least one way.)

Funerary Rites is not the same tale as the piper's or its conclusion. No rats were harmed in the writing of this story. I felt the base of it was the same as the Hamelin incident with its unanswered question:

Why *did* the children go off with the piper?

Could it be they felt the call of a life they preferred over the one they found themselves born into?

And wouldn't any one of us do this if we wanted to find the place where we might breathe more freely?

Even if few people from that past will understand what lured us outside the door in the first place.

❧

A reader wrote me after this story's first publication and asked why I didn't specify more about how the Smiths accomplished this enchantment of the villagers.

I had no answer.

Still don't.

How can I?

I'm still in my doorway wondering what's out there.

Just as I once was one of those who, when young, heard the sound of the parade outside and ran as if my life depended on it to happily join in, leaving the doorway of my first home, as well.

Best,

Douglas Clegg
March 27, 2019

ALSO BY DOUGLAS CLEGG

Want more signed and inscribed editions?
Visit DouglasClegg.com/signed-books

STAND-ALONE NOVELS

Afterlife

Breeder

The Children's Hour

Dark of the Eye

Goat Dance

The Halloween Man

The Hour Before Dark

Mr. Darkness

Naomi

Neverland

You Come When I Call You

NOVELLAS & SHORT NOVELS

The Attraction

The Dark Game (Two Novelettes)

Dinner with the Cannibal Sisters

Isis

The Necromancer

Purity

The Words

SERIES

THE HARROW SERIES

Nightmare House, Book 1

Mischief, Book 2

The Infinite, Book 3

The Abandoned, Book 4

The Necromancer

Isis

THE CRIMINALLY INSANE SERIES

Bad Karma, Book 1

Red Angel, Book 2

Night Cage, Book 3

THE VAMPYRICON TRILOGY

The Priest of Blood, Book 1

The Lady of Serpents, Book 2

The Queen of Wolves, Book 3

THE CHRONICLES OF MORDRED

Mordred, Bastard Son

COLLECTIONS

Lights Out: Collected Stories

Night Asylum

The Nightmare Chronicles

Wild Things

BOX SET BUNDLES

Bad Places (3 Novels)

Coming of Age (3 Dark Novellas)

Dark Rooms (3 Novels)

Criminally Insane: The Series (3 Novels)

Halloween Chillers

Harrow: Three Novels (Books 1-3)

Harrow: Four Novels (Books 1-4)

Haunts (8 Novel Box Set)

Lights Out (3 Collection Box Set)

Night Towns (3 Novels)

The Vampyricon Trilogy (3 Novels)

With more new novels, novellas and stories to come.

ABOUT THE AUTHOR

Douglas Clegg is the *New York Times* bestselling and award-winning author of *Neverland*, *The Priest of Blood*, *Afterlife*, and *The Hour Before Dark*, among many other novels, novellas and stories.

His first collection, *The Nightmare Chronicles*, won both the Bram Stoker Award and the International Horror Guild Award. His work has been published by Simon & Schuster, Penguin/Berkley, Signet, Dorchester, Bantam Dell Doubleday, Cemetery Dance Publications, Subterranean Press, Alkemara Press and others.

A pioneer in the ebook world, his novel *Naomi* made international news when it was launched as the world's first ebook serial in early 1999 and was called "the first major work of fiction to originate in cyberspace" by *Publisher's Weekly,* covered in *Time* magazine, *Business Week*, *Business 2.0*, *BBC Radio*, *NPR*, *USA Today* and more.

His book *Purity* was the first to be published via mobile phone in the U.S. in early 2001.

He is married, and lives and writes along the coast of New England.

Find the Author Online:

www.DouglasClegg.com

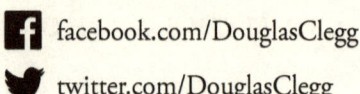 facebook.com/DouglasClegg

twitter.com/DouglasClegg